THE LLAMA'S SECRET

To my husband, Samuel Zeigler,
critic, helper, friend.

Library of Congress Cataloging-in-Publication Data

Palacios, Argentina.
    The llama's secret: a Peruvian legend / written and adapted by
Argentina Palacios; illustrated by Charles Reasoner.
      p.   cm.—(Legends of the world)
    Summary: A Peruvian rendition of the Great Flood story, in which a
llama warns the people and animals to seek shelter on Huillcacoto to
avoid the rising sea, Mamacocha.
    ISBN 0-8167-3049-0 (lib. bdg.)   ISBN 0-8167-3050-4 (pbk.)
    [1. Deluge—Folklore. 2. Folklore—Peru.] I. Reasoner, Charles,
ill. II. Title. III. Series.
PZ8.1.P17Ll 1993
398.21—dc20   92-21436

THE LLAMA'S SECRET

A PERUVIAN LEGEND

WRITTEN AND ADAPTED BY ARGENTINA PALACIOS   ILLUSTRATED BY CHARLES REASONER

TROLL ASSOCIATES

Long ago, high on a plateau in the Andes Mountains, there lived a man, his wife, and his children. The family had little: a small stone house, some food to eat, and a llama, their most prized possession.

In that harsh land, the family led a simple life, tending to their needs through hard work. Without their llama to help them, they knew they would have even less of the earth's bounty.

Day after day, the man and his wife loaded the llama with sticks and pails of water, and went out to work the land.

When the crops were harvested, they were taken back to the little stone house. The llama carried most of the load of *quinoa* grain, corn, and potatoes. The man, his wife, and his children carried the rest on their backs.

The man always provided his most prized possession with the best grass to eat. One day, he took the llama to the usual place, but the llama would not graze.

"Eat, *llamingo*, eat! Have your fill of *ischu*," the man implored. But the llama would not eat the grass.

Gently, the man placed his hand on the llama. He put his ear to its chest and said, "What is the matter with you? I do not find anything wrong, *llamingo*, but if you do not wish to eat, we will go home."

The man told his wife how the llama had not eaten any grass in the meadow. "Tomorrow, take him to a different place," said his wife. "Maybe the grass was not green and tender enough in that meadow. Perhaps, it was turning golden."

The next day, the man took his llama along a new path to another meadow. There, he examined clump after clump of *ischu* to be sure it was good enough to eat. But again, the llama would not graze.

For a third and fourth day, the man took the llama to meadow after meadow. On the fifth day, the man said, "*Llamingo*, if you do not eat today, you will get sick and die. You cannot die. I need you."

Instead of eating, the llama moaned — "Een, een," — and thick tears rolled down its face.

ONE OF THAT moaning and crying," shouted the man. "I am tired of your stubbornness. Must I whip you with this cornstalk to get you to eat?"

The llama looked up at its master. Quickly, the man stepped back, expecting the animal to show its annoyance by spitting, as most llamas do. Instead, to the man's amazement, the llama spoke to him. "My master, I cannot eat, for I know what I know. It is a great, great sadness."

"Aaaayyyy!" the man cried. "What do you know that makes you sad?" he asked.

"A terrible thing is going to happen. The world, as we know it, will come to an end."

"How do you know this, *llamingo*?"

"Mamacocha, the sea, has warned that great changes are coming," the llama replied. "She has threatened to flood the earth. She will drown and destroy everything in her path."

"Is there a way to save ourselves, *llamingo*?" the frightened man asked.

"Huillcacoto, the highest peak in the mountains, will escape the flood," said the llama. "Listen carefully, and do as I tell you. Go and get your family. Ask your wife to take enough food for five days."

The man ran home. The llama followed.

Outside his stone house, the man could see his wife spinning cloth from the llama's wool. The children were playing.

"Wife, we must stop everything," cried the man. "We must leave our home. A great flood is coming!"

"How do you know this?" she asked.

"Our llama has told me. Mamacocha is angry. She is going to flood the earth. We must go to Huillcacoto. There, we will be saved."

"Our llama has spoken?" cried the wife. "My husband, you have been too long in the hot sun." But when she looked in his eyes, she knew her husband was telling the truth.

So the man, his wife, and his children hurriedly dressed for their journey. Just as they were leaving, the llama reminded them to bring enough food for five days.

With the llama in the lead, they started their journey.

Soon, they came upon a herd of *guanacos*, grazing on a meadow. "A great flood will cover everything," the llama told them in their own tongue. "You must follow us to the peak of Huillcacoto."

The *guanacos* stared blankly at the llama.

"There is no time to waste," the llama continued. "Move quickly, or you will drown!"

At last, the *guanacos* understood and trotted up the slope behind the llama.

As the travelers approached a mountain lake, a flock of wading flamingoes sounded an alarm. "There is no need to fear us. We are not here to harm you," the llama told them in their own tongue. "But, beware! A great flood will cover the land. Save yourselves! Fly to Huillcacoto, the highest peak in the mountains."

The flamingoes took flight.

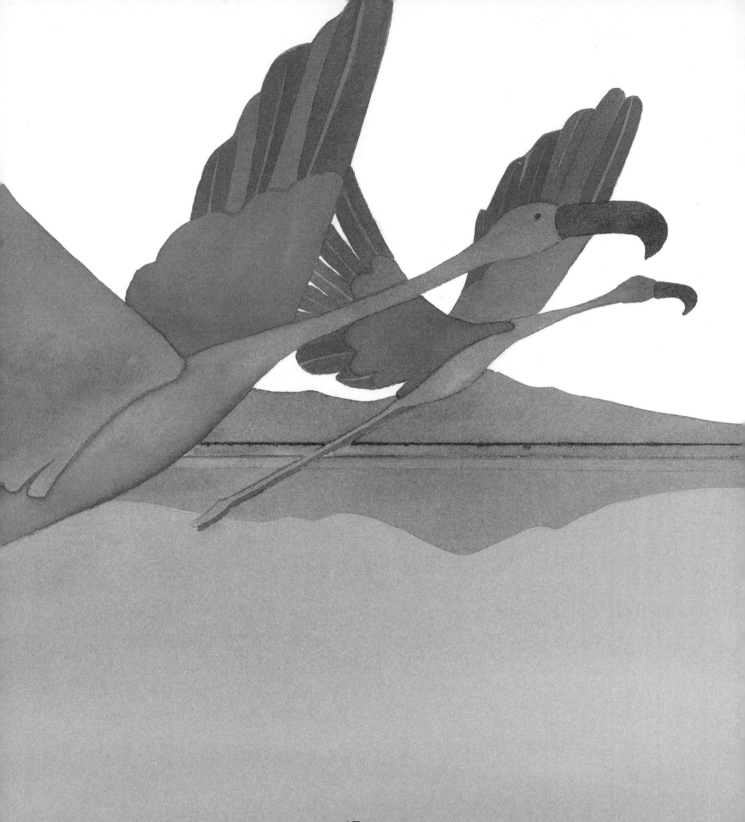

The climbers grew weary. They began to slow their pace.

"There is no time to rest," cried the llama. "Look! Mamacocha, the sea, is rising. If we stop, it will catch up with us."

So the travelers hurried on.

Now the group came upon a mother puma and her cubs. The mother was teaching the babies how to stalk prey.

"Stop," the llama told them in their own tongue. "There is no time to hunt. Mamacocha, the sea, will flood everything very soon. If you want to survive, come with us to Huillcacoto, the highest peak in the mountains."

The pumas listened, but all the while they were eyeing the other animals hungrily. "No, no!" cried the llama. "Behave. We are in this together."

Peacefully, the pumas fell in line and followed the llama up the mountainside.

Farther up, chinchillas were basking on the rocks. "Wake up," the llama said to them in their own tongue. "Mamacocha, the sea, will flood everything very soon, even these rocks. If you don't want to drown, follow us to Huillcacoto, the highest peak in the mountains."

The chinchillas understood. They soon followed the crowd.

A mother and father condor on a high rocky ledge were watching their baby try its wings for the very first time. When the llama told them, in their own tongue, about Mamacocha and the flood, they too headed for Huillcacoto.

Out of curiosity, a family of foxes came by to find out what was going on. They had never seen a procession of so many creatures before. The llama told them, in their own tongue, the story it had told everyone. But the foxes did not believe the llama's story, and they did not follow.

And so it went that the llama told each and every creature it met about the flood. The llama told them how to save themselves from it. Most listened and followed.

After a long, hard journey, they arrived at Huillcacoto. At the top, people and animals huddled together and watched the rising waters. "Look," cried the man, pointing toward the family of foxes they had seen on their journey.

"Hurry," the llama called out. The foxes barely escaped the rushing waters. They could find only a little room for themselves at the top of the mountain, so the tips of their long bushy tails had to remain in the water.

Suddenly, the sun disappeared. It became icy cold. Everyone was frightened. Until that moment, they had never known such darkness.

"Inti, the sun, has died," they all cried. "It has fallen from the sky into the waters. Mamacocha has swallowed it up!"

"Do not fear," said the llama. "The darkness will not last forever."

And then, just as suddenly, the sea stopped rising. As the llama had promised, the sky grew light once again.

"The sun has not died!" cried the people and animals.

"It was resting in the waters," the llama explained, "after many hours of hard work warming the earth and all its creatures. Do not be afraid! The sun will never die. Inti will always shine for us during the day. And, at night, while Inti is bathing, Mamaquilla, the moon, will come to cool us off and grace us with her beauty."

MAMACOCHA was satisfied. Her waters began to recede to the places where they can be found to this day.

Those gathered at the top of Huillcacoto began their descent. The first to climb down were the foxes, who now wore a black stain at the tips of their tails to mark the spot where they had touched the waters of darkness.

Today, in the Andes Mountains, there are people and animals who are the grandchildren of the grandchildren of the grandchildren of the ones who went to Huillcacoto. To show their gratitude, the people adorn their llamas with little bells and ribbons. They take them up to graze where the *ischu* is light green and tender.

While the llamas graze, the men play their flutes — their *quenas* and their *antaras*. The llamas, in turn, move their ears when they hear the music. That is the llama's way of expressing pleasure. For no llama has ever spoken in human words since that time so long ago.

The Llama's Secret is a legend from Peru, the third largest country in South America. Peru lies along the Pacific Ocean in the western part of the continent. While most of its large cities are along the coast, the Peruvian Andes Mountains lie east of that region, extending north to south down the length of the country. The story of the llama (pronounced YA-ma in Spanish) and the great flood takes place high in the Andes, where the Indians date back to the mighty Incas, who ruled Peru until the 1500s.

When the Spanish conquerors came to the region, the llama had been in existence for thousands of years. It was used to carry minerals, such as silver, from the mines.

Today, this sure-footed creature is most useful to the Andean people as a pack animal, transporting goods along mountain trails. The llama can carry up to 200 pounds (90 kg) on its back and can travel as far as 20 miles (30 km) in a day. It can live for weeks without drinking, getting the moisture it needs from green plants.

No doubt, the story of the heroic llama will have a familiar ring to anyone who knows the story of Noah and the ark. Flood stories are found throughout the world in cultures quite different from one another. This points out that people, regardless of their origins, are much the same everywhere.

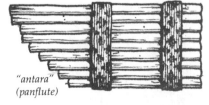

"antara"
(panflute)